A Note to Parents

Read to your child...

★ Reading aloud is one of the best ways to develop your child's love of reading. Read together at least 20 minutes each day.

★ Laughter is contagious! Read with feeling. Show your child that reading is fun.

★ Take time to answer questions your child may have about the story. Linger over pages that interest your child.

...and your child will read to you.

★ Do not correct every word your child misreads. Instead, say, "Does that make sense? Let's try it again."

★ Praise your child as he progresses. Your encouraging words will build his confidence.

You can help your Level 2 reader.

★ Keep the reading experience interactive. Read part of a sentence, then ask your child to add the missing word.

★ Read the first part of a story. Then ask, "What's going to happen next?"

★ Give clues to new words. Say, "This word begins with *b* and ends in *ake*, like *rake, take, lake*."

★ Ask your child to retell the story using her own words.

★ Use the five *W*s: WHO is the story about? WHAT happens? WHERE and WHEN does the story take place? WHY does it turn out the way it does?

Most of all, enjoy your reading time together!

—Bernice Cullinan, Ph.D.,
Professor of Reading, New York University

Published by Reader's Digest Children's Books
Reader's Digest Road, Pleasantville, NY U.S.A. 10570-7000 and
Reader's Digest Children's Publishing Limited,
King's Court, Parsonage Lane, Bath UK BA1 1ER
Copyright © 1999 Reader's Digest Children's Publishing, Inc.
All rights reserved. Reader's Digest Children's Books and All-Star Readers
are trademarks and Reader's Digest is a registered trademark of
The Reader's Digest Association, Inc. Fisher-Price trademarks are used
under license from Fisher-Price, Inc., a subsidiary of
Mattel, Inc., East Aurora, NY 14052 U.S.A.
©1999 Mattel, Inc. All Rights Reserved.
Printed in Hong Kong.
10 9 8 7 6 5 4

Library of Congress Cataloging-in-Publication Data

Mann, Paul Z.
    Meet my monster / by Paul Z. Mann ; illustrated by Maxie Chambliss.
       p.   cm. — (All-star readers. Level 2)
    Summary: A little girl tells all the reasons why she loves her
    monster playmate, even though he is really just pretend.
    ISBN 1-57584-308-0
    [1. Imaginary playmates—Fiction. 2. Monsters—Fiction. 3. Stories in rhyme.]
    I. Chambliss, Maxie, ill. II. Title. III. Series.
PZ8.3.M35535Me   1999   [E]—dc21   99-19688

Meet My Monster

by Paul Z. Mann
illustrated by Maxie Chambliss

All-Star Readers™

Reader's Digest Children's Books™
Pleasantville, New York • Montréal, Québec

Meet my monster!
Don't be scared.
Shake his paw. Say, "Hi!"

He isn't mean. He isn't fierce.
He is a little shy.

Mom can't see him.
Dad can't see him.
They don't think he's there.

But I can see him very well.
Just look at that blue hair!

My monster loves to play.
Me, too!

We love to play outside.

We run and romp.
We jump and stomp.

We climb.

We crawl.

We hide.

If it rains, we play inside.
I let my monster in.
We play with dolls.

We play with balls.
He always lets me win!

I like to paint
my monster's picture.
It's so much fun to do!

I paint him glad.

I paint him mad.
I paint him feeling blue.

My monster dances.
Watch him go!
He spins just like a top.

He drops.

He flips.

He taps.

He tips.

He never wants to stop!

My monster can be trouble, too.
He loses all my toys.

He makes a mess.
He wears my dress.
He makes a lot of noise.

He likes to watch TV with me.
He likes all kinds of shows.

He laughs.

He cries.
He rubs his eyes.

I help him
blow his nose.

My monster eats
things I don't like.
He eats string beans and beets.

He eats green peas.
He eats blue cheese.
He eats and eats and EATS!

My monster takes a bath
with me. We both sit
in the tub.

We splash and splish
like two big fish.
We scrub and scrub
and SCRUB.

My monster loves to read with me.
I read. He holds the book.

He loves the pictures most of all.
We look and look and LOOK.

My monster is a pest in bed.
He always steals the sheet.

He snores. He sheds.
He hogs the bed.
He kicks his big, cold feet.

But I don't care.
I need him there.

My monster is my friend.
I love him so. He doesn't know...

he's really just pretend!

Words are fun!

Here are some simple activities you can do with a pencil, crayons, and a sheet of paper. You'll find the answers at the bottom of the page.

———————— ★ ————————

1. Which word means the same as the word on the left?

glad (hot, happy, dry)

spin (loud, full, twirl)

shy (loud, bright, timid)

cold (chilly, nice, short)

mad (sour, easy, angry)

2. Find two words in the story that rhyme with:

toes

guess

zip

rub

sad

pop

3. What do we find out on the last page of the story? Can you make up a different ending?

4. Match the words that rhyme — even though they may not be spelled the same way.

romp	**shy**
glad	**blue**
hi	**feet**
sheet	**hair**
in	**mad**
there	**win**
do	**stomp**

5. The title of this book has an *M* in each word. Can you make a sentence with words that start with *S*? You can try other letters, too.

6. If you could have a monster for a friend, what would you do together? Draw a picture of your monster.

ANSWERS:
1. glad=happy; spin=twirl; shy=timid; cold=chilly; mad=angry
2. toes/nose/shows; guess/mess/dress; zip/flip/lip; rub/scrub/tub; sad/glad/mad; pop/drop/top
4. romp/stomp; glad/mad; hi/shy; sheet/feet; in/win; there/hair; do/blue